Disney's

Saturday Morning

abc

NO WIMPS ALLOWED!

Disney's One Saturday Morning host segments created by Peter Hastings.
Meme played by Valarie Rae Miller.

For information address Disney Press,
114 Fifth Avenue, New York, New York 10011-5690.
Printed in the United States of America.
First Edition
1 3 5 7 9 10 8 6 4 2
Library of Congress Catalog Card Number: 98-88402
ISBN: 0-7868-4307-1 (paperback)
For more Disney Press fun, visit www.DisneyBooks.com

NO WIMPS ALLOWED!

Starring your hosts
Meme & JELLY ROLL

The Lineup

Hey! Welcome to One Saturday Morning. You know, I keep thinking I'm forgetting something—something I'm supposed to do. Oh, well. I'll just put it out of my head, and relax, kick back, and enjoy, because here, it's Saturday, all book long.

What are you going to crush for us today, Jelly Roll?

A SUPER-DELUXE ROAST TURKEY DINNER.

Nice smushing, Jelly Roll.

Here's Pepper Ann.

Adapted by Barbara G. Winkelman.
Based on the original script by Matthew Negrete and Nahnatchka Khan.
Art by Brad Goodchild based on storyboard art by Wendy Grieb.

HAVE YOU EVER BEEN UNSUPERVISED?

Coach Doogan's seventh grade P.E. class stood around the pool. In bathrobes and swim caps, they listened as Coach Doogan introduced them to the wonderful world of diving!

"It's jumping, it's water, it's jumping into water—it's diving time!" expounded Coach Doogan.

She was pumped and ready to go, but the kids just stared blankly as she gestured at the diving board.

"Alrightee!" continued Coach Doogan. "Let's start with the low dive—or what I like to call the kiddie dive."

The kiddie

The kiddie dive! Pepper Ann said to herself. How cool!

"The kiddie dive?" asked Trinket out loud. "How lame."

Pepper Ann glanced around and saw everyone snickering.

She chuckled, too, and quickly changed her tune. "Yeah, lame. SOOO lame!"

Coach Doogan pointed to Pepper Ann. "Pearson! Start us off!"

Pepper Ann looked at her peers, who were stifling their laughter. She turned back around to face Doogan.

"Coach Doogan," she said, "I don't need to start with the kiddie dive. I'm ready for . . . the high dive."

"Sweet challah bread!" Coach Doogan cried. "The high dive is for experienced divers only!"

Pepper Ann took a deep breath, gritted her teeth, and said, "I'm ready!"

"Well, if you're really ready," Coach Doogan responded. "And your parents have signed the release forms . . . oh, why the heck not!"

"I'm ready for . . . the high dive."

Pepper Ann removed her robe with a flourish, and looked up. Towering above her was the high dive. It stood at least a thousand feet high. Pepper Ann started to climb the ladder. She could hear the cheers of Coach Doogan and her classmates as she ascended through clouds, past airplanes, comets, and even the space shuttle.

Pepper Ann finally reached the top. She walked out to the edge of the diving board, adjusted her suit, and turned her back to the water. Perfectly positioned, she gracefully leaped off the board.

Soaring down through the air, Pepper

Ann performed a triple back-axle slide and landed with a *plink* in the pool.

Wild cheers greeted her as she stepped out of the water.

"Beautiful!" Coach Doogan cried, teary-eyed. "Grab your duffel bag, we are headin' to the Olympics, Pearson. Oh, Pearson . . . Pearson! PEARSON!"

Pepper Ann opened her eyes. She was on the ladder to the high dive, twelve feet above the ground, and clutching the railing for dear life.

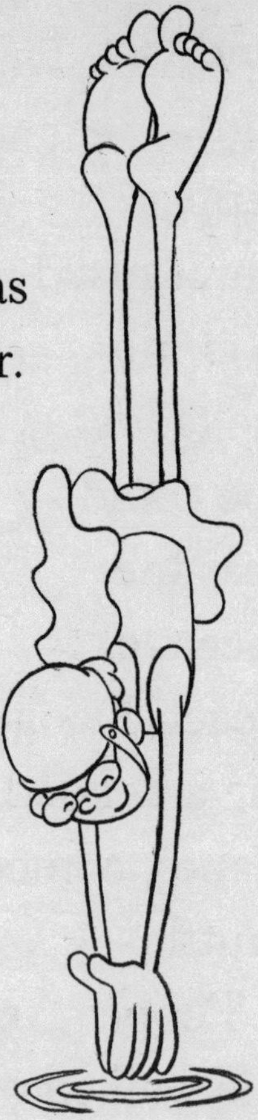

"HELP IS ON THE WAY!"

"Don't worry,"

Coach Doogan yelled through a megaphone from below. "Help is on the way!"

Pepper Ann could hear kids laugh-ing.

A fire truck, sirens blasting, raced up to the pool. It took them a few hours, but they finally plucked a terrified Pepper Ann from the high dive as they would a scared little kitten from a tree.

"You should have just said you weren't ready for the high dive," Nicky told Pepper Ann at lunch.

"It's not that I wasn't ready," said Pepper Ann. "The altitude made me light-headed.

After all, I was at least twelve feet high. I thought I handled myself with a lot of grace and dignity."

"Was that before or after you hurled in the fire truck?" asked Milo.

Before Pepper Ann could answer, Dieter stopped by and handed the three friends party invitations.

"Guten tag!" greeted Dieter. "I invite you all to my birthday party zis week-end. It is a Klaus-themed party. Klaus! Germany's favorite Jeep-driving *über*-monkey! I hope you all come."

After Dieter left, Pepper Ann turned to Nicky and Milo. "Dieter's nice and all, but aren't we a little too old to be having monkey-themed parties?"

Just then Tessa and Vanessa passed by, holding Dieter's invitations.

"I can't wait for . . . " said Tessa.

"This weekend," said Vanessa.

"Dieter's party will . . . " continued Tessa.

"Be the bomb!" finished Vanessa.

Two guys walked by from the other direction. They were also holding invitations.

"Whoa!" said one guy. "This party's gonna rock."

"Dieter's the Mack Daddy of hosts," said the other.

"Why is everyone so excited about Dieter's party?" Pepper Ann asked Nicky and Milo.

"Take a look at your invitation," Nicky answered.

Pepper Ann looked down at her invitation and saw in big bold letters: UNSUPERVISED.

"Unsupervised?" she asked excitedly. "As in we get to jump up and down on beds and go swimming right after we eat, unsupervised?"

"Unsupervised?" asked Milo. "As in we can watch TV an inch away from the screen, unsupervised?"

"Unsupervised," said Nicky. "As in free from supervision or scrutiny."

Pepper Ann and Milo stared at her in bewilderment.

Nicky shrugged. "Can I help it if I'm book smart?"

Trinket stopped at the table, and said, "Unsupervised, as

in kissing! Kiss City! Smoochville!"

Pepper Ann's mouth dropped open. She couldn't believe what she was hearing.

"Lip-lockin', house-rockin', spit-swappin', kissin'," Trinket continued.

"But unsupervised parties aren't supposed to happen until eighth grade," complained Pepper Ann.

Nicky shrugged. "It's a rite of passage. Like learning to walk, ride a bike, play Vivaldi's 'Autumn' on the viola."

Dieter approached them.

"So you come to my party?" he asked.

"Absolutely," answered Nicky.

"You bet," answered Milo.

They turned to Pepper Ann, who hesitated before answering. She felt as if everyone stopped what they were doing

to hear her answer.

Pepper Ann forced a weak smile and mumbled, "Sure."

Pepper Ann looked at her reflection in her helmet mirror as she Rollerbladed home from school.

"Why'd you say yes if you didn't want to go?" asked her reflection.

"What choice did I have?" Pepper Ann replied, throwing her hands up dramatically. "The entire seventh grade

"SOONER OR LATER," MOM SAID, "YOU ARE GOING TO REALIZE THAT LIFE IS UNSUPERVISED."

is going. If I don't go, everyone will think I'm a dork!"

Pepper Ann knew it was too late to back out of going, but then she had a thought:

There was no way her mother would let her go to an unsupervised party!

But even her mother didn't stop her.

"Sooner or later," Mom said, "you are going to realize that life is unsupervised."

Pepper Ann spoke to her reflection in the bathroom.

"First our parties are unsupervised, now my own mother decides to trust me.

My whole world has been turned upside down!"

"Easy, party girl," said her reflection. "Why are you so freaked out about this?"

"I've never kissed anyone before," Pepper Ann finally admitted. "There! I said it. Are you happy now?"

"Oh, come on," said her reflection. "How hard can it be to kiss?"

Pepper Ann imagined herself at the party. The place looked like a love lounge with velvet furniture and beanbag chairs. Love beads hung from the ceiling. A bunch of seventh graders, including Pepper Ann, played Spin the Bottle.

"All you need is a little practice."

A cute guy spun the bottle. It went around and around. Finally, it stopped. Right on Pepper Ann.

Everyone watched as Pepper Ann and the cute guy leaned toward each other from across the circle. As they got closer and closer, Pepper Ann's lips grew bigger and bigger. Everyone's eyes widened in horror. Big-lipped Pepper Ann swallowed the guy whole! And then she burped! Loud!

"All you need is a little practice," said

her reflection,
bringing her back to
reality.

"Of course!"
Pepper Ann cried.
"Practice!"

So Pepper Ann practiced. At the movie theater, she kissed her hand. At home, she kissed a cantaloupe melon. In her room, she kissed her teddy bear. Then she moved on to her pillow.

Finally, she was ready.

On the day of the party, Pepper Ann walked confidently beside Milo and Nicky.

But when she saw Dieter's

house, her confidence began to melt.

"There it is," Pepper Ann said, trying to hide her fear. "Dieter's house. The house of Dieter."

Nicky gave Pepper Ann a strange look.

Suddenly, Pepper Ann turned to her friends. "Wanna go over to Pizza Pit first?" she asked them. "My treat!"

"There'll be bratwurst at the party," Nicky replied.

"Wanna go see the rerelease of the Fuzzy trilogy?" Pepper Ann tried again. "Popcorn's on me!"

"We just saw it yesterday," said Milo.

"Pepper Ann," asked Nicky, "is anything wrong?"

"Wrong?" said Pepper Ann weakly. "What could be wrong? I'm fine. I'm fine and I'm ready."

Pepper Ann, Milo, and Nicky arrived at Dieter's house. When they walked in, Pepper Ann saw that her nightmare had come true! Dieter had transformed his living room into a love lounge. Pepper Ann gulped nervously. Dieter dimmed the lights and whipped out a soda bottle.

"Time for Spin ze Bottle!" shouted Dieter. "Everyone sit in a circle!"

Pepper Ann did what any normal twelve-year-old would do in that situation. She hid in a kitchen cupboard.

Nicky grabbed Pepper Ann and yanked her out.

Feeling doomed, Pepper Ann sat down in the circle next to Nicky.

The first player picked up the soda bottle. Pepper Ann looked at him in horror. It was the cute guy from her dream! He spun the bottle. Around and around it went.

It finally stopped . . . at her!

"Noooooo!" Pepper Ann cried as she leaped up from the floor. "I'm not ready! I thought I could do it because everyone else was doing it, but I can't. I like supervised parties and hopping off the kiddie dive. If that makes me lame, then I'm lame!"

"Pepper Ann?" Nicky gently called.

Pepper Ann looked at her friend.

"It's pointing to me," Nicky said.

Pepper Ann smiled sheepishly.

"Never mind," she said, wishing she could disappear into her party hat.

Nicky and the cute guy leaned toward each other across the circle.

Everyone watched as Nicky and the cute guy quickly kissed.

"Look, everyone!" shouted Alice Kane.

"Look, everyone!" She stood across the room among Dieter's birthday presents.

"Dieter got the new SuperMega-HardCore Gameblaster 8000!" she said.

The kids rushed over to check out Dieter's presents.

Spin the Bottle was over.

Later, Pepper Ann asked Nicky how the kiss was.

"It was okay," she replied. "But not nearly as exciting as my first sneeze! Did you know the power of one sneeze can literally cause one's heart to stop?"

Nicky rambled on about the wonders of sneezing as Pepper Ann just rolled her eyes.

As they walked home, Pepper Ann turned to Nicky. "Y'know, I might've

over-
reacted a little at
the party. All that birthday cake made
me light-headed."

Nicky and Milo exchanged glances.

"'Cause, if I did have to kiss some-
one," Pepper Ann concluded, "I would

have been fine. Totally cool. Completely ready—"

"Is that my little Peppie-schmep-pie?!"

Pepper Ann looked up to see her grandmother standing a few feet away, her arms outstretched.

"Come give your grandma a big kiss!"

Horrified, Pepper Ann turned to Nicky and Milo. "I take it back."

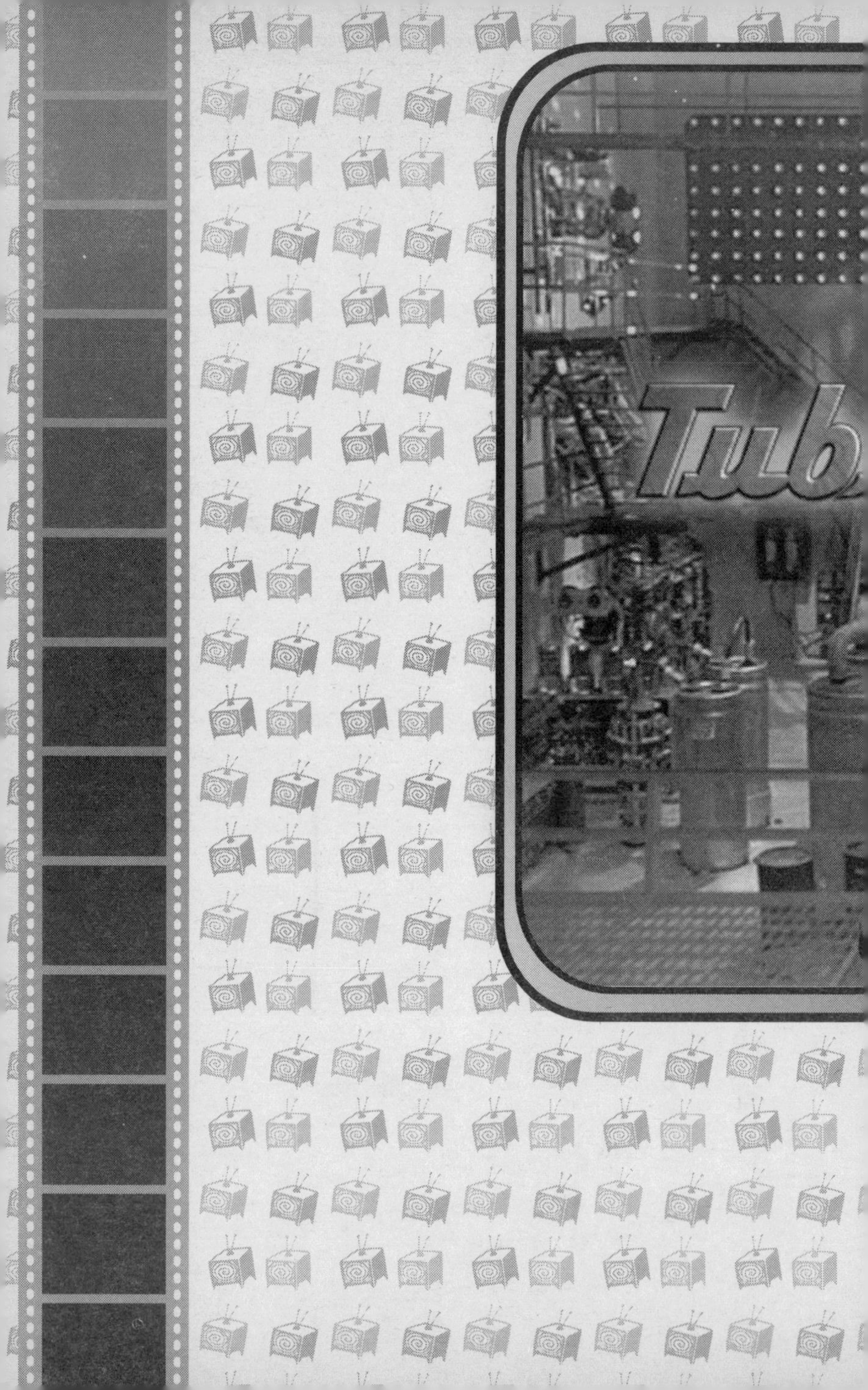

APPRECIATION

Based on the script written and performed by Peter Hastings and Paul Rugg.
Illustrations by Jim Ludkte.

Bob 1: "Oh, gee whiz."

Bob 2: "What?"

Bob 1: "I was just thinking about all the joy we bring, operating a television set."

Bob 2: "Oh, yeah, but not many people know that we're inside the television set."

Bob 1: "I know, they think it's the cable, or the wires, or the—"

Bob 2: "Or magic or something . . ."

Bob 1: "Magic TV!"

Bob 2: "But no, yeah, they're watching their shows. . . ."

Bob 1: "Just going and clicking their clickers."

Bob 2: "That's right, as we're working away in here . . ."

Bob 1: "Changing reels, making everything go, making sure the picture works . . ."

Bob 2: "Runnin' around for those people!"

Bob 1: "And they don't even know!"

Bob 2: "They don't even care!"

Bob 1: "You think they care?"

Bob 2: "No!"

Bob 1: "Do they care?"

Bob 2: "I don't know!"

Bob 1: "We think they care!"

Bob 2: "Well . . . some of them—yeah."

Bob 1: "Some . . . some of them care."

Bob 2: "Yeah, I think some of them . . ."

Bob 1: “There’s a lot of them.”
Bob 2: “Yeah, most of them . . .”
Bob 1: “A lot of them . . .”
Bob 2: “Most of them . . .”
Bob 1: “Care.”
Bob 2: “If not all of ’em . . .”

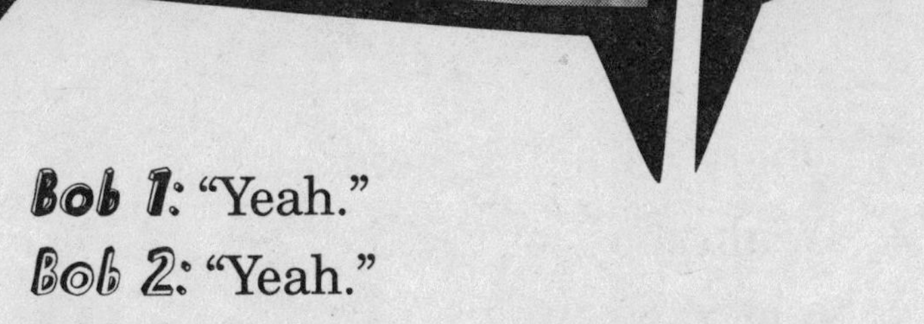

Bob 1: "Yeah."
Bob 2: "Yeah."
Bob 1: "They're . . . they're swell."

Hey, guys, welcome back. Don't stop reading now. The fun's just begun. Here's Disney's Doug.

Adapted by Judy Katschke
Illustrated by Kevin Kobasic.

Disney's

Doug™

Created by
Jim Jinkins

Doug Gets Right Back On!

Dear Journal,

The Rudolph Bluff Memorial Bike Rally and Bean Bake-off is Saturday, and Skeeter, Patti, Chalky, and I are determined to win that bicycle race. But with only a few days to go, things are looking bad. . . .

—from the journal of Doug Funnie

"I *will* be able to ride in the race, won't I?" Doug asked Dr. Dorsal.

"If Doug doesn't ride, I'll have to," Skeeter Valentine said. "And I'm slower than Christmas!"

Dr. Dorsal took the cast off Doug's leg. "How does the ankle feel?" he asked.

Doug wiggled his toes. He hopped around the room.

"Great!" he cried.

Doug's ankle was as good as new. Now all he had to do was fix his smashed-up, twisted bike!

• • •

Porkchop handed Doug a wrench.

"Thanks, Porkchop," Doug said.

"Rrr-uff!"

With the help of Porkchop, Doug was just a few spokes away from getting his bike on track.

"What's wrong with your bicycle, Douglas?" his neighbor Mr. Dink asked.

"I was training for the race," Doug explained. "And I ran it into a tree."

"The most important thing after a bike accident, Douglas, is to get right back on," Mr. Dink said.

"Shouldn't I fix it first?" Doug asked.

"Of course," Mr. Dink said. "But if you don't face your fears right away, they get bigger and bigger."

Doug listened as Mr. Dink told a story of his friend who was terrified of *beans.*

"It all started when my friend was a boy," Mr. Dink explained. "His uncle gave him a box of jumping beans. But they did more than jump. They were alive! And they had a very bad attitude!"

"Are we talking about beans, Mr. Dink?" asked Doug.

"Evil beans," Mr. Dink muttered as sweat poured down his face. "Since then, my friend has been afraid of beans!" he said.

"Beans? Like lima beans?" Doug asked.

"LIMAS?" Mr. Dink cried.

"Way to go, Porkchop!"

"AHHHH! WHERE??"

As Doug watched his neighbor dive into the bushes he suspected that Mr. Dink's friend was *really* Mr. Dink!

"Oh, well," Doug said. "Back to my bike."

But Porkchop had already finished the job.

"Way to go, Porkchop!" Doug said. "Now for a test drive."

Doug climbed onto his bike. He put his foot on the pedal. Then he froze.

Jumbo Street suddenly

became a terrifying hill—as high as Mount St. Buster! The tree he hit was creeping toward him with sinister limbs. Closer . . . closer . . .

"Hey, Funnie!" a voice sneered.

"AFRAID? YOU SHOULD BE!"

"Are you going to ride that piece of junk or what?"

"Huh?" Doug gasped. He looked up and saw Roger.

"What's the matter, Funnie?" Roger snickered. "Afraid? You should be! We'll beat you this year just like we did last year."

Doug's mouth felt as dry as cotton candy.

Maybe he *was* afraid. Not of racing Roger but of getting back on his bike!

• • •

Okay. So I walked my bike to school, Doug thought the next morning. It's a beautiful day for a guy to walk his bike to school. Besides, I'll ride it home!

Just then his friends rode up.

"You look like you walked the whole way," Patti Mayonnaise said.

"Walk?" Doug laughed nervously. "What kinda dope would walk a perfectly good bike to school? Heh, heh."

"AHHH-CHOOOO!" Chalky Studebaker sneezed.

"Coming down with something, Chalky?" Skeeter said.

Chalky sniffed. "A little cold won't keep me out of the race."

"That's the spirit!" Patti cried. "We're going to need one hundred percent from everybody on the team."

Patti was right, Doug thought. He would ride his bike again! He would do it for Patti! He would do it for the team!

"Um, right after school," Doug muttered.

At three o'clock Doug tried everything. He even tried covering his eyes. But it was no use!

"What? Are you afraid of your own bike?" asked Roger.

"Chicken!" Roger and his goofball

pals laughed.

"What a baby!"

"Maybe he needs training wheels!"

Being razzed by Roger and his gang was pretty bad, but worse than that, Doug thought, maybe Roger was right!

"Bike . . . crash . . . must ride," Doug mumbled in bed that night. When he finally fell asleep he had a bummer of a nightmare.

A bicycle monster loomed over Doug as a baby. The monster had claws for handles and sharp steely teeth!

"Bikey Man!" Baby Doug gurgled.

Doug woke up in a cold sweat. It was his worst nightmare ever—and it was practically true!

"B-B-BIKEY MAN!"

The day of the race couldn't come

slowly enough for Doug.

"We'll be cheering for you, Doug," Mrs. Funnie said. She loaded a pot of baked beans into the car.

Patti, Skeeter, and Chalky rode up on

their bikes.

"I thought we could all ride together, Doug!" Patti said.

Doug looked at Chalky. His nose was as red as a beet and as leaky as a faucet.

"AHHHH-CHOOOO!" Chalky sneezed.

"Chalky sounds awful," Patti whispered to Doug. "It's a good thing you're riding with us, Doug."

I can do this! Doug thought.

But as he neared his bike, it morphed into—B-B-Bikey Man!

Doug panicked. "I can't ride in the

race today!" he cried.

"What do you mean?" Patti asked.

Doug pointed to his foot. "My ankle hurts again."

"Wasn't it the—sniff—other ankle?" Chalky asked.

Doug had to think fast. "Er . . . the pain shoots from one ankle to the other!" he said.

Patti sighed. "That's okay, Doug. We'll just have to do our best without you."

Doug felt like a total loser. How could he let his best friends down?

He dragged his bike into Lucky Duck Park just as the bean bake-off was about to begin. He heard Mayor Tippy ask Mr. Dink, "Are you sure you want to judge the bean contest, dear?"

"Wife Tippy," Mr. Dink replied,

"judging beans is a lot like riding a . . . no, wait. Let me start over. Getting thrown by a bean doesn't mean . . . no . . ."

Tippy tried to help. "If you don't do it now," she said, "you'll never do it! Is that it?"

"Exactly!" Mr. Dink agreed. Then he entered the bean tent, muttering, "I'm bigger than beans . . . bigger than beans."

He took a whiff. Then he carefully sampled one tiny bean.

"Wow!" he shouted. "How can anything so evil taste so delicious?"

Doug watched as Mr. Dink scarfed down huge spoonfuls of beans.

If Mr. Dink can eat beans, Doug wondered, *why can't I get on my bike?*

Doug turned his eyes to the race. Patti's Pedal Pushers were up against

"ON YOUR MARK, GET SET," BANG!

Beebe's Butlers, Team Sleech, and Roger's Derailers.

"Be prepared to eat my dust again!" Roger jeered.

"On your mark, get set," *BANG!*

The gun went off. Patti took the lead in the first lap. Then it was Skeeter's turn.

"Go, Skeeter!" Doug shouted.

Meanwhile, Chalky was sneezing up a storm.

"AHH-CHOOO! AHH-CHOOO! AHHH-CHOO!"

Doug couldn't believe it. Every time Chalky tried to get on his bike, he sneezed himself off!

"I can—AHHH-CHOOO—do this," Chalky wheezed.

Doug wanted to help Chalky but he

couldn't even help himself.

"Doug?" Patti asked. "Are you okay?"

"No, Patti," Doug said. "I'm not."

Doug took a deep breath and told Patti everything.

"That was a pretty bad accident," Patti said. "It takes a lot of courage to get back on. But you're still a part of our team!"

By now, poor Chalky was crawling toward his bike.

"Can't let the team—AH-CHOO—down!"

That did it. Doug had to get a handle on Bikey Man, once and for all!

"I'm bigger than Bikey Man!" Doug repeated. "Bigger than Bikey Man!"

Doug gripped the handlebars. He pumped the pedals. Faster! Faster!

Faster—

"NOOOOOO!" Bikey Man screamed. But as Doug pumped the pedals, the monster's voice finally faded to nothing.

All at once, Doug's old bike was back. And Bikey Man was history!

"Way to go, Doug!" Patti cheered.

Doug passed Beebe's Butlers. He gained on Roger's Derailers.

"No way you're beating me, Funnie!" Roger snarled. He was so busy yelling that he missed the bridge!

"AAAAAHHHHH!"

SPLASH!

Only Al and Moo Sleech's solar-powered bike stood between Doug and winning. Until a dark cloud passed above.

"Oh, Hecuba! Shade is my doom!" Al moaned.

The crowd went wild as Doug sped through the finish line.

He wasn't a chicken, or a baby, or a loser.

He was a *hero*!

"We won! We won!" Patti, Skeeter, and a still-woozy Chalky shouted.

As his team carried him on their shoulders, Doug was the happiest kid alive. It had been a great day! They had won the race, his mom was named Bean Queen, and Mr. Dink finally ate beans . . . and he liked them!

"And I learned," Doug wrote in his journal, "that when you fall off your bean, you gotta look your bike in the eye . . . No, what I mean is, if your bike throws you off, you can't let the beans

. . . no, that's not it either. If you fall off the bicycle of life, you just have to face your bean in the face and say, 'Hey, I'm getting back on!' Or something like that!"

"Rowff," agreed Porkchop.

HOW THINGS WERK
WITH YOUR PAL
MR. WERKS!
ELEVATOR
Based on the script written by
Peter Hastings and Scott Gimple.

"Billy, put down the comic book and come to dinner!"

. . . "Elevators use a computer to signal motors attached to a series of levers and pullies. The elevator is attached to a metal track by wheels that allow it to easily slide up and down. . . ."

". . . The call-button in an elevator sends out coded instructions to headphones worn by the operators—giant, invisible retirees, several hundred feet taller than most buildings. . . .

. . . After these mammoth seniors decode their instructions, they push on the entire building, causing it to sink down. The elevator stays firmly in place, while the building itself is eased below ground level into a giant storage area called 'Chumkin's Bigabox' or 'Larry' for short. It's named after its inventor, Larry Chumkin. . . .

. . . After the passengers go on their merry way, the aged behemoth pulls the building out of Larry, and diligently awaits the next call. Levers and pullies? Nonsense! Just America's greatest resource—giant invisible retirees, and good old American know-how! . . .

. . The elevator, another Triumph of Industry!" . . .

Wow, you guys are a mess.
I know. What are we going to do?
Well, you could–
I think I have an idea.

"Wow!"

Water. I don't know who invented it, but thanks. Here's Recess.

Written by Judy Katschke.
Based on a television script by
Joe Ansolabehere and Paul Germain.
Original characters designed by
David Shannon.
Series art direction by Eric Keyes
Illustrations by Jose Zelaya, based on
storyboard art by Celia Kendrick.

Created by Paul Germain and Joe Ansolabehere

The New Kid

"Miss Grotke?" Gretchen called, raising her hand.

"Yes, Gretchen?" Miss Grotke said. "Do we have a problem?"

"No, Miss Grotke," Gretchen said quickly. "I'm quite clear about light . . . and no light."

She held up a healthy plant and a dead plant.

"But I'm more interested in the effects of

nitrogen-enriched soil," Gretchen said. She held up an even bigger plant! "Then of course there are other mixtures. Like a fifty-fifty nitrogen . . ."

Miss Grotke's eyes glazed as Gretchen rambled on . . . and on . . . and on!

All systems go! T. J. thought.

Vince raced to Miss Grotke's desk. He opened the drawer and pulled out THE KEY!

Vince tossed the key to Spinelli. She turned to Mikey and nodded. Mikey and a group of kids quickly formed a human pyramid.

Spinelli scampered to the top. She popped the key into the clock. Then she turned the big hand to the right. Nine-fifteen . . . nine-thirty . . . nine-forty-five . . .

Spinelli gritted her teeth as she carefully pushed the hands to ten!

R-R-R-R-RING!!!

"Recess already?" Miss Grotke asked. She looked at the clock and shrugged. "Everybody dismissed."

LIKE A PIT BULL IN ARMY BOOTS

T. J. and the gang led the stampede to the door. They swung it open. But just as they were about to spill into the hall, they stopped short.

A soldier stood outside the door. He looked big and mean, like a pit bull in army boots. He puffed out his big barrel chest.

"Miss Grotke?" he barked. "Lt. Griswold USMC reporting to deploy my son!"

"Deploy?" Miss Grotke squeaked.

"Yes, ma'am," Lt. Griswold said. "My boy, Gustav, has been assigned to your barracks—I mean—class."

Vince turned to T. J. "Any guy named Gustav is bound to be trouble."

"Priv-ate, report!" Lt. Griswold shouted. He stepped aside. A small, geeky kid stood behind him.

Mikey's jaw dropped open.

"That's Gustav?"

T. J. stared at Gustav. He wasn't at all like his dad.

"Why don't you tell us a little about yourself, Gustav?" Miss Grotke asked.

Gus pushed his glasses on his head. He knew the routine.

"My name is Gus," he said. "I've been to twelve schools in the past six years."

Yawn!

"Uh, Miss Grotke?" Willie asked. "Can we go to recess now?"

Miss Grotke nodded. "Why, certainly," she said.

Gus looked confused. "Excuse me, but isn't it too early for recess?" he asked.

"Well, no," Miss Grotke said. "We always go to recess at ten."

"But it's only—"

T. J. threw his arm around Gus's shoulder.

"Come on, Gus!"

T. J. said. "I'll show you around!"

"You know the rules of the playground."

"Over there's the jock section," T. J. explained as they walked through the Third Street School playground. "They give nasty wedgies—"

Suddenly Vince grabbed T. J. by the arm.

"Uh, T. J. Could I speak to you in private?" he asked.

"Sure," T. J. said. He turned to the rest of the gang. "You introduce Gus to the Bug-Eating Kid. We'll catch up."

When they

were finally alone, Vince turned to T. J.

"You know the rules of the playground," he said. "You're not supposed to talk to a kid like that for at least forty-eight hours!

"What do you mean, a kid like that?" T. J. asked.

"You know," Vince whispered, "a . . . new kid."

"If I don't say anything, and the rest

of the class doesn't say anything," T. J. said, "who will know?"

Then they heard it. The sound of beating drums filled the air. Kids dropped to their knees and bowed.

T. J. made Gus bow, too.

"HALT!" KING BOB SHOUTED.

A troop of big guys marched through the playground. Some of them carried a kid on their shoulders.

"Who's that?" Gus whispered to T. J.

"King Bob. He runs the place," T. J. whispered back. "Whatever you do, don't say you're a—"

"HALT!" King Bob shouted.

The procession screeched to a stop.

T. J. and the gang held their breath as King Bob stared down at Gus.

"Who are you?" he demanded.

"I'm a new kid," Gus said.

King Bob flashed an evil grin.

"We haven't had a new kid around here lately," he said. "Where's the old New Kid?"

A pale boy with hollow eyes stumbled through the crowd. "Here I am, Your Highness," he stammered.

"You are no longer the New Kid," King Bob told him. "From now on you are . . ."

A guard checked the tag on the back

"We have a NEW New Kid."

of the old New Kid's undershirt.

"Morris P. Hingle," he read.

"Right!" Bob declared. "You are Morris P. Hingle again!"

Morris began kissing King Bob's ring.

"Oh, thank you!" he sobbed. "Thank you!"

"Watch the ring," King Bob snapped.

Then he pulled Gus up and held him high.

"We have a new New Kid," King Bob shouted. "From now on he will be

known as the New Kid and nothing else!"

Gus listened to the crowd. Being a new kid couldn't be that bad. Could it?

"Out of the way, New Kid!"

It was Gus's first full day as the New Kid. If he could only get on the school bus!

"Come on, New Kid," Bertha, the school bus driver, sneered. "I don't have all day!"

Gus dragged himself onto the bus.

"Where am I going to sit?" Gus asked, since all the seats were taken.

A kid pointed to a lonely seat in the back. It was marked NEW KID.

There was no escape for the New Kid. Not even during recess! When

they lined up to choose teams for kick-ball, everyone was picked before him. Even the kid with a cast on his leg.

"Uh," Gus said in a shaky voice. "What about me?"

"Oh, sorry," a team captain said. "But according to the Constitution of the Playground, Section Three, Paragraph Two under Kickball—NO NEW KIDS!"

It was more than Gus could take.

"I'm nothing but a loser," Gus groaned the next day. "See you guys later, if I don't shrivel up and blow away first."

Gus walked away, muttering to himself.

"That kid is really starting to bug me!" Spinelli snapped.

Mikey turned to Spinelli. "How

would you feel if they took away your name?" he asked.

Spinelli thought about it and gulped. She was tough, but not that tough.

The gang felt hopeless. Then, suddenly, T. J.'s eyes lit up.

"Hey!" he cried. "Maybe we can help him!"

The gang watched T. J. pace back

and forth like a tiger in a cage. He had another plan coming on!

"When we're finished," T. J. said, "he'll never be the New Kid again. He'll be . . . he'll be . . ."

T. J. turned to the gang.

"What was his name again?"

It was early the next morning. Gus trudged his way to the school bus. Suddenly, T. J. and Mikey appeared behind him.

"How's it goin', Gus?" Mikey asked.

"Oh . . . fine," Gus said, surprised.

"Looks like a beautiful day," T. J. said. "Eh, Gus?"

Gus stared at T. J. and Mikey. Did they just say . . . his name?

Just then the school bus pulled up. When the doors opened, Gus noticed

something strange. Bertha was smiling!

"Hop on the bus, Gus!" Bertha said with a grin.

Gus climbed aboard. His eyes popped wide open. The kids on the bus were smiling at him, too!

Gus turned to T. J. "What's going on here?" he asked.

T. J. shrugged. "Why, nothing's

going on . . . Gus!" he said.

Gus sat down and looked out the window. Then he gasped.

"Right this way, Gus."

There was an enormous billboard on the road. It read: GOOD MORNING GUS!

The bus pulled up to the school.

"Right this way, Gus," Willie said, holding out his hand.

Gus started to walk toward the school, but he didn't get far.

A kid unveiled a statue of Gus. Gus choked back a sob as a giant banner was dropped over the school. It read:

3RD ST. SCHOOL
WELCOMES GUS!

"Gee," Gus said as a brass band marched by. "Maybe I am somebody. Maybe I really do have a name!"

The world was suddenly a beautiful place for Gus Griswold. Until . . .

"It's the king!!!"

The kids froze as the drumbeats got louder and louder. Then they scampered around like bugs on a hot plate.

Gus watched in horror. Everywhere he looked his name was replaced with—NEW KID!

"You guys all know me," Gus said to one kid after another. "Billy? Rachel? Clarise?"

The kids looked down sadly. Then they turned away.

Gus whirled around to T. J. and the gang.

"I AM NOT A NEW KID!" "You guys know who I am, right?" Gus cried. "Right?"

"How can we know who you are," T. J. asked, "if you don't know who you are . . . NEW KID?"

"I am not a New Kid!" Gus screamed. "I am a human being!"

"Don't tell us," T. J. said. He pointed to King Bob. "Tell him!"

Gus stared at King Bob.

"Okay," he said slowly. "I will."

The crowd parted for Gus as he walked toward the sixth-grade hulks.

"Gus . . . Gus . . . Gus," the kids chanted softly.

Gus jumped in front of King Bob's guards. He put his hands on his hips.

"Hey!" King Bob shouted. "Who's blocking the way down there?"

He looked down at Gus.

"Oh, it's *you*, New Kid," King Bob said. "Move aside."

"Not this time, Bob," Gus said.

"What?" King Bob boomed. "You can't talk to me like that!"

"Oh, yeah?" Gus cried. "Well . . . just watch me!" A hush fell over the playground.

"All my life, I've been treated like a nobody," Gus shouted. "Just because I

"I am GUS P. GRISWOLD!!!"

was the New Kid! But then I came to this school, and for the first time in my life, I was like a friend."

Gus pointed his finger at King Bob.

"Then you come along and make me a nobody again," he snarled. "Well, you listen to me. I am not a nobody. I am GUS P. GRISWOLD!!!"

King Bob looked bored. "So . . . what's your point?" he asked.

"I want my name back!" Gus yelled.

King Bob shrugged. "Okay," he

said coolly.

Gus stared at King Bob.

"That's . . . it?" he asked.

"What do you want, a parade?" King Bob cried. "You got your name back. Now get out of here!"

I got my name back, Gus thought. "You hear that, everybody?" Gus shouted to the kids. "I got my name back!"

T. J. and the gang ran over to Gus.

"I've got a name!" Gus cried as the kids hoisted him onto their shoulders.

Just then a kid burst through the crowd. It was Morris P. Hingle.

"It's not fair!" Morris told King Bob. "He was the New Kid for only a few days. I had to do it for three whole years!"

King Bob leaned back on his throne.

"Hey," he said to Morris. "You should have said something."

Morris was in shock. Then he broke down and cried.

But no one seemed to hear poor Morris. They were too busy parading Gus through the playground.

"GUS! GUS! GUS!" the kids chanted.

Gus grinned from ear to ear. He wasn't the New Kid anymore. He finally had a name. It was Gus P. Griswold!

BOSS
OF THE
WORLD
RANDY

"Hi, I'm Randy. I'm ten years old. This is what I'd do if I were boss of the world. . . .

. . . If I were boss of the world, I'd fly—because it's—I hate going in a car—it's so boring, it's dull—and

walking, your legs get all, like, tingly and stuff, but if you're flying, it's like you're nice and cool and peaceful. I'd fly like a *peregrine* falcon. I'd be—I'd feel great—really great—I'd feel like I'm special. . . ."

Thanks for stopping by One Saturday Morning. See you next time.

REMEMBER: PRACTICE ACTS OF RANDOM KINDNESS ON SATURDAYS.

Bye!